Captain Maximillem
Stori

Anne Loraine Johnson

MAPLE
PUBLISHERS

Captain Maximillem Stories

Author: Anne Loraine Johnson

Copyright © Anne Loraine Johnson (2022)

Illustrations Copyright © White Magic Studios

The right of Anne Loraine Johnson to be identified as author of this work has been asserted by the author in accordance with section 77 and 78 of the Copyright, Designs and Patents Act 1988.

First Published in 2022

ISBN 978-1-915164-25-4 (Paperback)

Book cover design, Illustrations and Book layout by:
White Magic Studios
www.whitemagicstudios.co.uk

Published by:
Maple Publishers
1 Brunel Way,
Slough,
SL1 1FQ, UK
www.maplepublishers.com

With love to my Grandchildren and thanks to my husband and family for all their encouragement

CONTENTS

Part 1

A Stolen Map and a Grizzly Bear

It all began with a map, a map stolen from some poor unsuspecting pirate enjoying himself so much in a tavern that he didn't even notice it was gone! Taken by pirate captain, "Maximus Maximillem", unaware of the precarious journey that the map was about to lead him on.

He had visited the shore disguised as a vagabond, so not to be recognised as a pirate captain. Very soon after stealing the map he left the tavern and was barely able to contain his excitement! He began rowing as fast as he could out to his ship left anchored far out in the bay. With thoughts of finding lots of treasure circulating around his head now, having almost reached his ship, he was to gleefully wave his prize in the air for all to see!

After scrambling on board as fast as he could, Captain Maximillem now began bellowing for his pirates to raise the anchor and hoist the sails. "Make haste, hurry, hurry", he screamed at them, "there's treasure afoot, we're setting sail now and if you lazy lubbers don't get a move on, there'll be no more rations for any today!" Hearing this, very soon, the "Black Rigg" was on her way.

It was most unfortunate that the men that had been chosen to join him on the Black Rigg, about twelve, all did seem rather cowardly. Having been discreetly enlisted in various taverns they had been tempted by promises of finding lots of treasure, adventure and excitement, along with plenty for them to eat and drink.

Not very tall, rather rotund and having tiny electrifying icy blue eyes was to all make him look extremely mean, it was little wonder the pirates were weary of him. Hearing tales told that not long ago he had made some poor souls walk the plank indeed was only to have absolutely terrified them! Aware of there being enormous fish and man-eating sharks in the high seas, it had come as a great shock to them having been told there was too, a giant sea serpent!

Captain Maximillem became the proud owner of his pirate ship having won her in a wager with a pirate captain. Painted black all over, apart from just one narrow yellow stripe round her, as her name suggests he immediately renamed her "Black Rigg". At this time, although rather old and creaky, she had seemed to be quite seaworthy.

Having set sail in such haste Captain Maximillem now had become anxious about others finding the treasure first. With this in mind he was bellowing for his men to sail faster "go faster, faster, hurry up you lazy lubbers," he was screaming at them, also relishing, "I wonder which one of you will walk the plank today?" Hearing this, terrified of being in a sea with sharks, let alone a giant sea serpent, his men really had no other choice given to them than to work harder. However, it is doubtful any would have walked the plank, as fewer men would only lead him to working harder himself!

Worryingly, it was now several weeks since setting sail with no sightings of any land and weather each passing day turning colder. Even the most timid of the men, tired and hungry, was starting to grumble. Fed up with their captain, most of them regretted ever joining him. All leading an angry Captain Maximillem questioning the treasure map truly to be one. Venting his bad temper on his men, accusing them of not following instructions, he was shouting at them, "Whoever I find out is to blame for this, will be left on the next island we come across!"

As if matters could get no worse, Captain Maximillem having hastily ordered the Black Rigg set sail, he had completely forgotten all about loading his ship with extra supplies. Sadly, all left now were just a few ships' old dry biscuits with a half barrel of ale being rationed! There was still plenty of rum to be drunk but this on empty stomachs was a very bad idea!! Greedy Captain Maximillem, not intending to starve himself, had made sure that safely stored away in his cabin were more than a few tasty morsels!

Thankfully any dissatisfaction the men had turned out to be short lived as it was only a few days later that a faint outline of an island appeared on the horizon. Hoping that, at last, this would turn out to be the island, all aboard the Black Rigg now were greatly excited!

As they drew closer to the island, Captain Maximillem had spied that not very far away was a small fishing boat. Having seen this, immediately he gave the order to drop anchor and launch the jolly boat. The men were then told to go seize and bring back all the fish caught by the fishermen. Squashing themselves into a small narrow rowing boat they soon set out.

Returning, the pirates were soon to unload a large net full of fish onto the deck of the Black Rigg. Hooray! At long last there was plenty of food on board for all!! Sadly, the fishermen, taken by surprise, were left fleeing back to the safety of their homes. Today, there would be no fish for them to sell or feed their families with.

That night on board the Black Rigg, an order was given for the fish to be served up in the galley. Then with full stomachs and plenty of rum being drunk all made merry. Indeed, it turned out to be a most noisy affair with all stinking very much of fish!

Early the next morning once again the fishing boat was to appear. But today, Captain Maximillem had bigger fish to fry – firstly, finding the treasure! Besides, there was still more than enough fish left for everyone.

With his men feeling a bit under the weather having sore heads from the previous night's merriment, all now in the jolly boat were heading for the island. First to land on the island leading the way, Captain Maximillem began shouting at the men to make haste, waving the treasure map in one hand and his rusty old sword in the other. "Make haste, you lazy lubbers, keep up," he screamed. The weary pirates, unable to keep up, unfortunately, now were lagging far behind, leaving him striding ahead all on his own.

Charging forth, Captain Maximillem then suddenly caught sight of something to make him stop in his tracks. Letting out a loud shriek, dropping the map and his rusty old sword on the ground in fright, he quickly turned around in order, along with his men, to run as fast as he could back to the jolly boat. But oh dear, his men, with none having given any thought to arming themselves were now nowhere to be seen! They, too, having seen what had frightened Captain Maximillem so much, headed straight back to the safety of the Black Rigg. He was now left all alone on the island!

What they had all seen was the largest grizzly bear one could ever have imagined, who upon smelling Captain Maximillem stinking very much of fish, knocking him to the ground was pressing a large foot down on his chest! Captain Maximillem, hardly able to breathe, was much too frightened to even shout for help. It did seem that very soon he was to be eaten up by the grizzly bear. Absolutely terrified, having dropped his sword too far away to defend himself, he was smelling the grizzly bear's fishy breath sniffing all over his face!

All of a sudden there was the sound of something being dropped from behind the grizzly bear heard. Upon hearing this, the grizzly bear immediately turned around, releasing Captain Maximillem from its clutches. Much to his relief and astonishment two men had suddenly appeared, one quickly picking up his sword and both dragging him down to the water's edge where there was a fishing boat waiting to carry them to safety.

For Captain Maximillem it had been extremely lucky the fishermen he previously stole the fish from, having watched him and his pirates head towards the island took advantage of it being safe to fish again. Aware of a large grizzly bear somewhere on the island, it was after seeing the pirates fleeing for safety without their captain, they had realised something to be very wrong.

Thankfully the fishermen turned out to be kindly men who, attempting to save Captain Maximillem had brought all the fish caught in their nets with them, throwing it to the grizzly bear. As hoped, smelling the fish the grizzly bear then quickly released him. Of course, what must have alerted the grizzly to a feast was when all the men approaching the island had been very much stinking of fish!

Sitting in the fishing boat taking him back to the Black Rigg was a very subdued, embarrassed pirate captain. Not only cross not to have found any treasure, but absolutely furious with his men for leaving him alone on the island! None of these lazy lubbers shall be eating any more fish or drinking rum today. "No, they'll all be eating the ship's dry old biscuits and working through the night scrubbing the decks till they sparkle!" he said, fuming to himself.

As soon as the fishing boat reached the Black Rigg, Captain Maximillem, hurriedly clambering on board immediately ordered that all the stolen fish that was left be returned to the fishermen. Although, it has to be said, being so mean and greedy, before any of the fish was returned, he did make sure that just a few were kept back for himself!

In sombre mood the pirates returned all the fish to the fishermen. It was then Captain Maximillem, checking first that none of his men would overhear, thanked the fishermen for saving him, promising he would not steal their fish ever again.

But would Captain Maximillem really be able to keep his word?

Captain Maximillem and Captain Jacque du Plomp

After his unfortunate meeting with the grizzly bear, wasting no time at all, Captain Maximillem immediately issued orders for the Black Rigg to set sail. Still fuming after being abandoned on the island, hoping to reach warmer climes, he began to scream at his pirates "turn the ship round we're heading south, get a move on!" He could not get away fast enough from the grizzly bear island as not only had it been bitterly cold, but probably had been the last place to find any treasure! It truly was the most unpleasant island he had ever set foot on!

Once sailing again, it was not long before the opportunity arose to plunder an unsuspecting ship. Resulting in now there being not only a handsome cargo of supplies on board the Black Rigg, but to Captain Maximillem's delight, also a large haul of gold and silver coins!

With the Black Rigg now sailing in warmer seas, Captain Maximillem was spending most of his time peering through his telescope looking out for more ships to plunder. But it was late one afternoon peering out to sea he was to spot something to greatly alarm him! On the horizon coming into view and seemingly fast approaching, was a brightly coloured red ship heading straight towards the Black Rigg!

Having heard stories told about a gaudy red ship and a strange pirate captain he was now about to meet him in person.

11

Known as "Captain Jacque du Plomp", he did remember briefly catching sight of him on a recent shore visit, thinking him to look a bit of a toff and far too posh to be a pirate captain. A tall statuesque figure, he had looked extremely vain, dressed flamboyantly, with short blonde hair neatly coiffed and wearing jewellery. But oh dear, worst of all, he was known to wear perfume!

Captain du Plomp's pirate ship, being not a very large ship, was painted a vivid red colour. Captain Maximillem thought this absolutely ridiculous! No, no, a pirate ship never ever should be recognisable on the high seas! He thought Captain du Plomp to be a real "dandy"!

It was thought Captain du Plomp came from a wealthy family living in the West country whose parents having given him a fine education, despairing of his lazy ways, bought him a ship so as to go seek his own fortune. To keep him safe, a handful of their faithful servants had been entrusted to look after him.

Captain Maximillem certainly did not wish any of his men ever to meet this unusual pirate captain. But oh dear, it did now seem that here he was in his outrageous ship tracking the Black Rigg! What on earth could he do?

Not really wanting to fight Captain du Plomp, not because he was afraid, but hoping the Black Rigg would be able to out manoeuvre the gaudy ship, Captain Maximillem immediately ordered his men to hoist another sail. "Hurry, whatever happens we mustn't be caught up with" he shouted at them. But alas, all was too late now with it looking to be just a matter of time before he was to reach them! Captain du Plomp was now to be seen clearly standing at the helm of his ship with his telescope focused on the Black Rigg! Never had there been such an urgent need of a plan to stop him!

"Carry on men, sail faster, faster," Captain Maximillem screamed to his men before hastily disappearing down to his cabin. Picking up some discarded parchment paper he found down on the floor and finding a small piece of charcoal quickly he drew a map of three islands. By carefully marking one island with a black cross, to then make the map look really old he dropped it down on the dirty floor. By sprinkling one or two drops of ale over it, he then in his dirty old boots jumped up and down on his map, all to make it appear very old.

Checking his rusty old sword was safely at his side, grabbing a handful of gold and silver coins he had safely stored in a treasure chest, after hurriedly putting them in a money bag and tying it tightly round the neck, he then rushed back to join his men on deck.

Captain Maximillem had hatched a cunning plan involving an island he knew very soon they would be passing by. An island he had visited not very long ago in search of treasure, only to make a very hasty retreat after finding it to be infested with giant rats!

He planned to entice Captain du Plomp as near to the Black Rigg as possible, but to achieve this he needed his men to take early to their beds. "Busy day tomorrow for you lazy lubbers," he screamed at them, "to your beds now!" Worn out having worked so hard the men seemed only too pleased to obey. Left alone to navigate the Black Rigg he planned to slow her down to almost a standstill in the hope of Captain du Plomp attempting to board her.

Seeing the gaudy red ship fast approaching, Captain Maximillem now was hearing music coming from it. Then, drawing closer he heard a most ridiculous song was being sung - "Ho, ho, ho, with a bottle of rum, what a jolly time I'm having, oh what fun!" Hearing this only confirmed what he already thought!

All a bit of a gamble should Captain du Plomp try to board the Black Rigg, it was Captain Maximillem's intention to fool him. He would pretend to be frightened and thought a coward. He would offer up a bag of coins to try and make him go away, but at the same time try to draw his attention to him hiding something behind his back. Hopefully he would then be forced to show what he was trying to conceal (the treasure map) and made to hand it over. Would Captain du Plomp then rush ahead in order to find the treasure first?

The very thought of Captain du Plomp and his men visiting the island only to find giant rats brought a rare smile to Captain Maximillem's face. Yes, if all went well his plan looked to be an excellent one!

Hooray, hooray! It all had seemed to have worked perfectly well! With his plan set in motion, Captain du Plomp had fallen for it hook, line and sinker! Having almost boarded the Black Rigg from a small boat by climbing up the side he had flashed his sword around high in the air. However, anybody witnessing this spectacle, him trying hard to look menacing, rightly so would have thought him a real fool! Captain Maximillem, gritting his teeth, bent on playing his frightened cowardly role must too have looked rather silly, especially with Captain du Plomp not even noticing him trying to hide something behind his back. In fact, it had resulted in him, along with the bag of coins, almost having to hand it over! As Captain Maximillem had suspected, Captain du Plomp proved himself to be not quite so clever after all!

The following day was when the Black Rigg was to sail past the island that had been marked with a cross. Passing the island was when all were to see anchored not far away from it Captain du Plomp's gaudy red ship. But, oh dear, the most dreadful rumpus was to be heard coming from it! Captain Maximillem's pirates all being unaware of his crafty plan, upon hearing loud shrieks and thrashing about sounds were now left to wonder - what on earth was going on?

Trying hard to not let his men see the large grin now growing across his face, Captain Maximillem, could only tell them he knew about giant rats being found on the island but not about any monkeys!

Old Ned who along with his Pirate Ship was there and then not?

Leaving the noisy rat-infested island far behind, still looking to find more treasure, Captain Maximillem and his men continued their journey. As to where they were heading, nobody knew for sure, this being just the way Captain Maximillem liked it! However, it should always be remembered sailing into the unknown very often could turn out to be foolhardy, as Captain Maximillem and his men were all about to find out!

It was late one night when having sailed for many days that the Black Rigg suddenly found herself in some extremely stormy waters. Mountainous seas so rough only very few experienced pirate captains with their sturdy ships could have survived and where sadly many ships' captains along with their crews would have perished.

A howling gale force wind was blowing with deafening thunder and lightning strikes continually lighting the skies with their blue and red flashes. Torrential rain thundered down on the decks of the Black Rigg now creaking very badly, rocking violently from side to side making it all very difficult for anybody to stay upright. It now most certainly was a case for all hands on deck, and for any pirate happening unfortunately to be suffering from sea sickness, a truly horrific experience!

The storm raged on and on throughout the night keeping the pirates extremely busy bailing out water likely to make the Black Rigg sink and harnessing down anything sliding around the decks and likely to be swept overboard. It was a most unpleasant time for all, but not so for Captain Maximillem who after giving orders was disappearing to his cabin to partake in some tasty morsels and the odd drop of rum. No, Captain Maximillem certainly had no intention to let a seemingly unpleasant storm get in the way of any of his comforts!

It was on one of his trips back up on deck that he was to see something to make him stop him in his tracks. Straining his eyes, peering out on the stormy seas with the skies still constantly lighting up, he had caught sight of a faint outline of a ship. Surely, he thought to himself, "Could it be Captain du Plomp they had left far behind when sailing past the rat-infested island? How on earth was it possible he had caught up with them?"

Puzzled, pointing in the direction where he thought he had seen the ship, he immediately ordered two men busily working nearby to look out to sea and tell him whether they could see anything.

But it was after a while having stood very still straining their eyes through the mist, both afraid they were in trouble, could they only report seeing rain falling down.

Perplexed, now Captain Maximillem, standing at the bow of the Black Rigg, did wonder whether he in fact had seen the mysterious ship. Maybe it was a trick of the light, but then adding to his confusion he did think he too had heard the sound of an eerie bell ringing out? But with all the noises going on, pirates shouting to one another, thunder and lightning strikes, howling winds with heavy rain pounding the decks, he might well have been mistaken.

As fast as the storm had raged there was a sudden calm, with, apart from two men left on watch, everybody taking to their beds.

The following day, all seemed to be back to normal as the Black Rigg continued on her journey. Allaying Captain Maximillem's worries to whether the mysterious ship seen the previous night had been Captain du Plomp's, a ship had suddenly appeared on the horizon. But it was upon closer inspection and much to Captain Maximillem's relief that he was to realise the ship looked nothing like a gaudy red ship. And so, with happy thoughts of yet more treasure to be found, Captain Maximillem immediately gave the order for his men to go plunder it.

Having found the unfortunate ship's crew to not have put up much of a fight, the pirates very soon returned with plentiful supplies and a handsome haul of gold and silver coins. All on board the Black Rigg now were very happy, with especially Captain Maximillem having yet more treasure!

The following night a fine mist was beginning to fall over the Black Rigg once again making the decks damp and slippery. But with the sea remaining calm and no signs of a storm brewing up, apart from two of them, all the pirates were given permission to take to their beds. However, this particular night Captain Maximillem to enable him to navigate the ship himself, with two keeping watch, decided he would stay up himself. Uneasy after the previous night's sighting of the mysterious ship, he still was anxious should his men ever meet Captain du Plomp. Secretly he was very worried it might well have been him seeking revenge for the giant rat trick.

The fine mist that had been falling earlier was very quickly now turning into dense fog with once calm seas becoming rougher and rougher sending at least ten feet high waves crashing down on the Black Rigg. It was then that it happened again! Whilst peering through the heavy mist Captain Maximillem had caught sight of the faint outline of a ship. Hearing the sound of an eerie bell ringing out was leaving the pirates on watch trembling in their boots.

Worried, Captain Maximillem ordered his two men to wake the sleeping pirates up telling them to be up on deck immediately, armed and ready to fight! Half asleep, the pirates having been hurriedly

awoken soon scrambled up on deck to join Captain Maximillem who was peering through his telescope.

All stood still in the rain and fog waiting for something to happen. With only sounds heard of pirates' trembling legs clattering and an occasional muffled cry, through the now thinning fog there appeared the outline of a silvery shimmering ship. It was then with the sound of an eerie bell ringing that all were to see dressed in old fashioned pirate clothes standing at the helm of the shimmering ship, the tall figure of an elderly man.

Looking anxiously in the direction of the Black Rigg the elderly man holding high a dimly lit lantern was frantically waving to her and pointing. It seemed that he was desperate the Black Rigg should change course and steer away from where she was heading. Alarmed, Captain Maximillem with no time to lose then began to bellow as loud as he could that the men were to change course.

It was not long after the Black Rigg had been hurriedly steered away that the sea was to grow calmer with the dense fog gradually lifting. However, it was now with dawn just breaking when Captain Maximillem was to see exactly where they had all been heading! It was to his horror with the realisation of what danger they actually had been in, he was looking at a large group of extremely dangerous jagged rocks!

Captain Maximillem could only wonder now whether a story told of a pirate captain named "Captain Ned" known only to appear in extremely stormy seas saving pirate ships in peril, actually was true!

Not wanting to believe tales of a ghostly pirate captain, who many years ago one particular stormy night, sailing on the high seas had perished alongside his crew, Captain Maximillem began to scan the sea with his telescope. He saw nothing.

Feeling slightly uncomfortable, just in case it had been Captain Ned they had all seen, Captain Maximillem making sure none of his men would see, sent a special pirate captain's salute out to sea thanking him!

A Mystery Island with a Big Surprise

After having encountered such stormy seas the Black Rigg thankfully now was sailing much calmer waters with the weather gradually growing hotter and hotter. For the pirates attempting to keep themselves cool, life on board was most certainly no fun. Mean Captain Maximillem was continually keeping them busy, working them very hard scrubbing decks again and again, polishing the masts, cleaning sails and plucking carbuncles off the anchor. There too was the jolly boat needing repair after seemingly taking in water every time it had been launched. Sadly, all this work left the men to dream of what it might be like relaxing in the sunshine.

Having no intention himself to work in such extreme heat, Captain Maximillem now was spending most days lazing around in his hammock basking in the sun. His pirates, upon seeing this spectacle, were understandably becoming very angry, with even two slightly braver men talking about jumping ship whenever land was reached!

Unfortunately, as he often did, Captain Maximillem had set sail without any particular route to follow, with nobody on board having the faintest idea where they were heading. All that did to be happening now was that sailing on day after day, it was becoming considerably hotter!

Each day for the men seemed to be turning into the day before, working hard, eating, drinking ale and rum and then going to bed. Even Captain Maximillem was bored now with doing the same old things.

Issuing orders from his hammock, devouring lots of tasty morsels, drinking plenty of rum and at bedtime tossing a coin as to which two pirates would be on lookout! Becoming lazier and lazier, it was all he could do to bother giving any orders to his men, and with plenty of supplies still left for everyone, even to order a passing ship to be plundered!

With it being several weeks and still no sightings of land, the pirates now were starting to get angry. Hungry and thirsty and with the Black Rigg's once plentiful supplies beginning to run out, they also were becoming frightened. Even two of the slightly braver men were now contemplating jumping ship whenever land finally was reached! But thankfully for Captain Maximillem just before any mutiny could take place, it was a few days later the men were to spot on the horizon, what at first glance had looked to be not a very large island.

Greatly excited, to at long last have sighted land, the pirates now had become extremely noisy. Noisy enough to arouse Captain Maximillem sleeping close by in his hammock, who grabbing his telescope from his coat pocket and surveying the land, immediately issued orders that the men sail close to the island.

What he had seen through his telescope, was an island that had looked to be a most pleasant one. He spied an abundance of fruits, bananas, coconuts, pineapples, oranges with lots of colourful vegetation, some of which had never been seen before and now awaiting the jolly boat to be launched, he could hardly contain his excitement, with thoughts of maybe yet more treasure to be found!

Much looking forward to stretching his legs after having been at sea for so long, just before anybody was to go ashore he did issue a word of warning to his men to all proceed with caution. "There could well be enemies and dangerous animals", he bellowed to his men, "be on your guard and ready to fight!" It was then having dropped anchor, checking for his rusty old sword to be safely at his side, that the jolly boat was launched with all heading for the mysterious island.

Drawing closer to the island, Captain Maximillem was to suddenly "hush" his men. Whilst focusing his telescope on the island he had caught sight of something that had puzzled him. He had seen some rather oddly dressed men watching their approach but when he looked again had disappeared. Worryingly, he could now only think them to be hiding somewhere.

Daring not to mention what he had seen to his cowardly men, knowing full well they would flee straight back to the safety of the Black Rigg, Captain Maximillem warned them that they might well not be alone on the island. "Stay close to one another, keep eyes sharp and your wits about you" he began bellowing to them.

First to set foot on the island after safely securing the jolly boat was Captain Maximillem, who now puffing out his chest in grandeur was waving his sword in the air, leading his men along a white silvery beach heading towards some dense undergrowth.

Reaching the dense undergrowth all heard lots of giggling excited sounds now coming from it. Stopping in their tracks, Captain Maximillem's thoughts were, there must be foreign people hiding away. It was then in a panic he began to shout, "Men, be ready to fight, there are enemies afoot". Of course, hearing this, all his men were simply terrified!

It was not long then that out of the dense undergrowth there suddenly appeared a group of strangely dressed people. Tall, scantily dressed men with their faces painted, wearing brightly coloured feathers in their hair and ladies in colourful, unusual clothes with children screaming and dancing around them in their excitement seeing the new arrivals.

Captain Maximillem behaved as he normally did whenever confronted with something he was not too sure about! Puffing his chest out in grandeur and taking off and on his floppy old hat. Waving his rusty old sword in the air he then at the top of his voice began shouting, "I am here to take over the island!"

Wondering whether the strangely dressed people understood one word of what he had said, Captain Maximillem was then taken by surprise by two men suddenly lurching towards him and grabbing his arms, making him drop his sword on the ground. Holding tightly, they then began frogmarching him towards a not very large, drab looking mud hut. "Let me go, let me go," Captain Maximillem screamed in alarm, "Men, help me, help me, help me fight off these wild men!" Alas, Captain Maximillem's plea only fell on deaf ears, his men being now far too preoccupied, fussed over by some pretty ladies with excited children handing out delicious fruits and tasty treats for them.

Poor Captain Maximillem, the strange men had thrown him into the drab looking hut and had left him in the sweltering heat for what seemed to be hours. Adding to his misery, there was only a rough old wooden box for him to sit on and now being extremely hungry and thirsty, nothing for him to eat or drink.

Not very far away he could now hear laughter and merry making sounds that seemed to be coming from his pirates. "Just wait until I get out of here," he thought to himself, "those lazy lubbers will pay for leaving me and not even attempting to rescue me!"

At long last underneath a gap in the door of the hut, food and drink consisting of a small piece of unappetising dry old meat and hollowed out coconut shell of milk was passed through to him.

Quickly grabbing the food and drink, feeling slightly better, Captain Maximillem then immediately commenced to shout and scream to be set free. But all was to no avail and after a short while, weary and hoarse from shouting, he finally grew quiet. Then with night fast approaching all there seemed left for him to do was to lie on the floor to try and rest.

The following morning Captain Maximillem awoke to hear lots of excited shrieking and banging and clattering sounds. Once again, he bemoaned his imprisonment, shouting at the top of his voice that he should be set free!

However, it was not long before the door to the hut was suddenly flung open, with two strangely dressed men grabbing him by the arms and marching him in an ungainly fashion towards a large exotic looking hut.

Reaching the exotic hut Captain Maximillem then saw that his pirates were all standing around cheerfully chattering to each other. Seeing this spectacle made him absolutely furious! But before there was any chance to bellow at his men, there, standing at the entrance of the hut appeared a tall statuesque figure, dressed in vivid coloured silks.

Captain Maximillem's usually ruddy face now turned ashen! Surely, he thought this couldn't be Captain du Plomp? But oh dear, it most certainly was, for there was no mistaking his blond coiffed hair!

After greeting Captain Maximillem with a note of sarcasm, Captain du Plomp was then to enquire whether or not he had had a pleasant night. Captain Maximillem, unable to contain his anger, growled at him, telling him that as he was a pirate captain he had no business locking him up! Captain du Plomp much amused, then hastened to add he also was a pirate captain, but was being looked after by and living with the island people.

Captain Maximillem's thoughts now were: was Captain du Plomp seeking revenge for the rat trick that had been played on him? But it was then that Captain du Plomp was to go on and tell him that should he wish to be set free, he would have first to agree on doing something for him.

Captain Maximillem, not used to being bullied into doing something he didn't want to do, could now only listen to what he had to say. Captain du Plomp told him he was intending to stay with the people on the island but that his trusty servants were in urgent need of returning to England so as to report back his wellbeing to his parents.

Captain du Plomp proposed that Captain Maximillem take his servants back home in the Black Rigg, explaining although he still had his own ship in case it should be needed again, it was safely hidden out of sight on the other side of the island. Then he went on to tell Captain Maximillem after having spoken with his pirates, only three had wanted to return home to their families. In truth, the pirates now very much enjoying themselves with the island people and particularly the young ladies all wanted very much to stay!

Hearing all this in indignation, Captain Maximillem's face turned a vivid red. "What an ungrateful lot of lazy lubbers," he began shouting at his men! This, leaving Captain du Plomp to look on in amusement, knowing only too well the men's reasons!

Having no other choice than to agree to Captain du Plomp's proposal if he wished to be set free, after having his rusty old sword returned to him, plans were hurriedly made for a hopefully safe passage back to England.

Later that same day Captain Maximillem, his three pirates and the five trusty servants set out to board the Black Rigg in a jolly boat fully loaded with supplies. All unaware of the grave danger the voyage they were about to embark on would involve them in.

Is it to be a Disaster for the "Black Rigg"?

All seemed well at first for the Black Rigg journeying back to England, sailing in calm waters with the weather still warm. But things were not going quite so well for Captain Maximillem! The three pirates returning home after having met Captain du Plomp were very much braver and no longer prepared to work as hard as they used to. This was now leading him having to do a lot more work himself with certainly no time for any lazing around! Knowing he really needed their help, however, he dared not risk upsetting them!

He now had to contend with Captain du Plomp's trusty servants proving not at all seaworthy men, mostly ignoring orders and refusing mundane jobs for fear they might get their clothes dirty! How on earth they were ever of any use to Captain du Plomp, he did wonder. Although it has to be said, the Black Rigg seemed much tidier, and there were some very tasty morsels now being served up in the galley! So maybe, they might be proving a tiny bit useful!

After sailing around three or four weeks it was early one morning when Captain Maximillem peering out to sea as he normally did suddenly noticed a group of large sea creatures swimming next to the Black Rigg. Instantly recognising them as swordfish, dolphins, maybe porpoises, basking sharks - hopefully that were not man-eaters, and not very far away a pod of spouting whales. Not unduly worried, having seen all these before, it was what happened next that really set the alarm bells ringing! Out of the corner of his eye he had caught sight of something swishing around in the air that looked like an enormous green tail, to then quickly disappear beneath the water!

With the Black Rigg beginning to creak badly and rock violently from side to side, Captain Maximillem noticed all the large sea creatures seen previously to have vanished. Now in a state of panic he immediately ordered for the Black Rigg to be steered as far away as possible from where he thought he saw the green tail. He had just one thought in mind, "Were they sailing in seas with a giant sea serpent?"

Later, that day having safely sailed away from the green tail sighting was showing signs of a storm brewing up. As each hour passed the sea grew darker with more and more white caps appearing. Heavy rain had begun to fall with a strong wind blowing up. In the distance, rumbles of thunder could be heard, indicating the lightning strikes to follow.

Familiar with the signs of a storm brewing, Captain Maximillem was to straight away give orders to the pirates to batten down everything likely to move around the decks. Deeming it a waste of time he didn't bother asking the trusty servants standing forlornly on deck, anxiously surveying the skies, for any help.

Did they not realise the seriousness of a bad storm? Captain Maximillem began growling at them to get out of his way and let him get on with battening down the decks. "Get down below, you lazy lubbers," he shrieked at them, "there's a storm brewing and I don't need the likes of you, useless lot hanging around hindering me!" Slightly embarrassed, muttering to themselves, not used to being spoken to in such terms, all left for them to do was to quickly scurry down below decks.

The storm, as all the signs were showing, was turning out to be a particularly nasty one, in fact even worse than the one when Captain Ned was sighted. This time, Captain Maximillem really felt the Black Rigg, now listing badly due to the heavy rain thundering down on her, to be in danger!

Knowing that he had been left with not nearly enough hands to man the decks, Captain Maximillem now regretted leaving most of his men behind with Captain du Plomp. But had he really had any choice? Perhaps he should have treated them a little better? But with no time to dwell on such things, convinced what lazy lubbers they had all been, it was good riddance of the lot!

Just when things could have gotten no worse, the pirates frantically steering the Black Rigg creaking and veering from side to side, were all to see heading straight for them, the most terrifying sight! Turning Captain Maximillem's legs to jelly and making the men scream and run for cover, was the most enormous green sea serpent! A sea serpent so large, up until now any tales told by seafarers, very likely would only ever have been half-believed!

Hearing a rumpus, the trusty servants below decks now popped their heads up to find out what was going on, only then to quickly disappear having seen the serpent. Captain Maximillem, trying hard to control his temper, could only think them to be truly cowardly! But with no time to waste on what he thought, reaching for his rusty old sword, in a vain attempt to scare off the monster, he began bravely to thrust it above the serpent's head.

Becoming very angry, the serpent now was lashing its tail against the hull of the Black Rigg almost making her capsize, then after briefly disappearing under the sea was returning again and again to lash out at her. Mortified, desperate to save his ship, Captain Maximillem saw through the splintered wood at the hull there was a small gaping hole appearing!

Oh dear, how could he save the Black Rigg with him having only four men to help fight the serpent off? Or, so he thought. Suddenly the trusty servants were back on deck throwing large portions of meat and fish with the odd copper pan or two, in fact, anything they could find at the sea serpent! They even managed to find one of Captain Maximillem's safely stored away treasure chests to throw overboard! Several barrels of rum were being tossed overboard with one hitting the sea serpent on the head stunning it and breaking into pieces spilling out its contents.

Sailing as fast as they were able, to get away from the serpent, the pirates thankfully had recovered a little from their fright. But it was all very strange as they seemed to be well outmanoeuvring it and were seeing it in the distance swaying from side to side in a most peculiar fashion! There now was a huge sigh of relief heard on board! Somehow, they had managed to outwit it.

Captain Maximillem did acknowledge the trusty servants for having helped him, as indeed this time they really had made themselves useful! What puzzled him though, was, why the sea serpent suddenly had left them alone?

There was one likely explanation, though! Could it have been that the serpent, attacking the barrels, piercing holes in them and releasing the contents into the sea, taking a liking to the taste of the rum and drinking it, have become quite disorientated?

After the sea serpent scare with the hole in the hull temporarily repaired, soon the Black Rigg once again was on her way back to England with understandably all on board still on the lookout for sea serpents!

With most of the supplies having been thrown overboard, all now had to make do on very meagre rations, with greedy Captain Maximillem absolutely hating this! However, everyone was only too aware just how lucky they had been surviving the sea serpent!

After several uneventful weeks land was finally sighted, most likely France, not England. Awareness that very soon the journey would be coming to an end now left Captain Maximillem to ponder on what he and the Black Rigg should do next.

His very first priority would have to be attending to the makeshift repair of the Black Rigg. He would have to make sure of course she did not attract attention to being a pirate ship, knowing that whenever he visited a port, it was always very dangerous. His intention was to be especially careful accompanying his pirates and the trusty servants back to shore, leaving the Black Rigg anchored far out at sea with the pirate emblem flag carefully hidden away.

We know that Captain Maximillem whenever visiting a port always went in disguise, for it was vital nobody should discover him to be a pirate captain. Being only too aware that if any port authority person ever suspected him of being one, it would most certainly end his seafaring days, seeking treasure and plundering ships. The very thought of being thrown into jail with maybe his life at stake or being sentenced to hard labour ending up in some far away unpleasant land, truly terrified him!

Knowing there were plenty more ships to be plundered and treasure found, he intended immediately to find a pirate crew. And this time, he would make sure they were only brave men who were always ready to fight off enemies! No, there most certainly would be no room on the Black Rigg for any cowardly men, only very, very brave men!

To his dismay and anger, even after they actually had helped him save the Black Rigg he was furious that the trusty servants had disposed of one of his treasure chests. All he now could think of was to find a replacement to fill again with treasure, but this time, he would make sure it was hidden away where nobody would ever find it!

Although most unlike him, Captain Maximillem after all that had happened recently, in order to prevent disloyalty from his men, was now to realise he might well need to treat them a bit better. Was he about to change his ways? Well, maybe, or maybe not!

Part 2
Urgently Required - New Pirates

Arriving safely back safely in England after almost losing his pirate ship along with most of his treasure, fighting off the giant sea serpent, Captain Maximillem after hurriedly having repaired his ship was now looking to find a new crew. This time however, he would be choosing only the bravest of men. They would be nothing like the ones he had left behind with Captain du Plomp. Yes, now only the very bravest would do!

Disguised as a vagabond once again he would go ashore visiting various taverns and persuade enough men to make up his crew. As before, promising lots of treasure, plenty to eat, excitement and adventure, he trusted, would do the trick.

In urgent need of recouping his supplies and his lost treasure, Captain Maximillem was now only too aware how badly he needed a new crew to plunder unsuspecting passing ships. Putting anchor down close to a port was always an anxious time for him should somebody raise the alarm seeing a pirate ship in the vicinity. The Black Rigg now urgently needed to be on her way.

Captain Maximillem's luck did seem to be in, though, for it did not take him very long to find at least twelve brave men. Hopefully, they were to be much more reliable than his previous "lazy lubbers".

After setting sail with plentiful supplies a few days later, it had become noticeable to Captain Maximillem, one of the men, a tall slithery sharp-eyed, jet black haired, pirate called "Jake", was showing signs of being troublesome. Not caring the least, he had been bossing around the other men, all seemingly in awe of him.

As by now the Black Rigg was well on her way on the high seas, all left for Captain Maximillem to do was to ensure he was kept an eye on. He decided by only giving him very mundane jobs this might humble him, making him realise exactly who was the Captain of the Black Rigg! Putting him to work below decks, to cook and clean, yes, that would sort him out!

With Jake safely below decks being kept an eye on, continuing their journey they were to have come across more than a few unsuspecting ships to plunder. Reaping copious rich rewards, things now seemed to be looking up for him!

Although content with the way the voyage had been progressing so far, Captain Maximillem still felt vexed by the behaviour of the slithery, very sharp-eyed Jake. Arousing his suspicions at meal times, just out of ear shot he was furtively speaking with the other pirates, sharing secrets. Witnessing this now, caused much annoyance to Captain Maximillem.

It was then at one meal time with most pirates present, Captain Maximillem no longer able to contain himself, demanded to be told what they had all been discussing. As expected, Jake, the first to speak, told him about an island close by where he knew there to be bountiful treasure hidden. Hearing this, a furious Captain Maximillem demanding as to why he had not been told about this, ordered Jake at once to draw a map leading them to the island.

"Whenever there's treasure afoot, don't any of you dirty lubbers dare not to tell me," he bellowed at them. "You're all on rations now for the rest of the week!" Giving Captain Maximillem a surly look, Jake quickly rose to his feet and with a smirk across his face, disappeared. Very soon he returned, holding in his hands a scrap of paper upon which was a map showing where the treasure would be found.

After having heard there was treasure to be found, Captain Maximillem immediately ordered that the Black Rigg be sailed as fast as she could.

Captain Maximillem finds himself to be in deep trouble!

Following Jake's directions, it was not long before land had been spotted and the Black Rigg's anchor put down. But just before the jolly boat was launched, to Captain Maximillem's surprise, Jake politely informed him it might be better to visit land under cover at dusk. Normally not listening to any advice from a subordinate, thinking perhaps it was a good idea, all on board awaited darkness to fall.

With it now being the middle of the afternoon awaiting it to grow dark was almost too much for Captain Maximillem to bear, leaving him only to imagine any riches awaiting him!

At long last with darkness having almost fallen across the Black Rigg, Captain Maximillem and his men, apart from two he left on board, set off in the jolly boat. The night was still and calm whereupon just before approaching land they saw two distant, faint lights. Reaching land, shushing his men to keep quiet, tethering the jolly boat between rocks, they then all stepped onto land.

Beckoning Captain Maximillem, Jake then showed him exactly where the treasure was to be found. Just as he had said, now in front of him he was looking at not just one wooden crate but at least half a dozen! With sharp, dark eyes flashing and glinting in great excitement, Captain Maximillem ordered all the crates to immediately be loaded onto the jolly boat. But he then was suddenly confronted by an alarming sight!

Standing before him were four uniformed burly men armed with pistols. Before realising what was happening to him, with three of his men not quick enough to have got away all were arrested. With hands tethered behind their backs they were then all dragged off and thrown into an old cart. "This will teach you dirty little smugglers," one shouted to them "We've been on the lookout for you for a long time!"

After being bundled into the cart everything suddenly fell into place. Jake had tricked him and he had fallen for it! All left for him now was either a lengthy jail stay or something very much worse..... he was now to stop his thoughts, it was all becoming too unbearable to think about.

The journey in the cart not a long one, took them along an extremely bumpy road. Captain Maximillem and his men all bound together then found themselves being pushed down a very cold, dank narrow passage. Upon now hearing the sound of water constantly dripping they were then to arrive at a large wooden door. The door then was flung open by a guard and all were thrown into a cold, dark, high walled room with an out of reach iron barred window, only just large enough to let a small amount of light in.

Never had Captain Maximillem been so cross or felt so miserable. Cross at having been duped by Jake, he now thought of him as "Jake the Snake", and miserable being incarcerated with men he felt to be inferior. Did they not know he was a pirate captain? Attempting to tell them this was met with much laughter and a rude jeering song. Adding salt to his wounds he now knew what the smuggled crates were to have contained, tea, wine, spirits and lace were most definitely not what he thought to be treasure!

For Captain Maximillem with his men, it was a ghastly time now having been imprisoned for what did seem to have been months in a smelly rat-infested wet cell. To prevent starvation, they were enduring the most revolting food, surviving on some kind of meat stew, hopefully not vermin, with a few small pieces of hard stale bread. Their drink was no better, being given a large jug of dank seemingly dirty water to be passed to one another. How Captain Maximillem dreamed of the rum and ale and all the tasty morsels he had kept for himself!

After several more miserable weeks it was early one cold wintry morning when to everyone's surprise a key was heard put in the lock of their heavy iron door. The door then was flung wide open. All being tethered together, Captain Maximillem along with his men and several others now were led along a dark narrow passageway. Reaching the end of the passage all were pushed up a narrow flight of stairs to find themselves herded into a big airy room where sat at a large foreboding table was an elderly sour-faced man dressed in a uniform.

In next to no time all the prisoners including Captain Maximillem were to have been sentenced by the sour-faced man to serve at the very least ten years' hard labour. Immediately they were to be taken down to the nearby harbour and put on a ship waiting to transport them across the seas.

With the anger he felt towards Jake the Snake growing, all Captain Maximillem could do now was to accept his fate. Oh, how he wished he had made Jake the Snake walk the plank, this was all his doing!

Reaching the harbour, they were all loaded onto a large old ship where, shackled together, they were pushed into a large iron container deep down in the hull. Captain Maximillem could only think that this was to be his very last voyage.

A Most Horrible Place to be in

Day in day out Captain Maximillem and his men were working long hours. Made to break rocks in extreme heat, they began at first light, finishing at dusk. They were building a wall around the island incarcerating them with each passing day making it look more and more like a fortress. As to where they actually were, Captain Maximillem had no idea and didn't care! None were left with any choice but to work hard, especially with the guards always on the lookout for any slackers, ready to shout and knock them around.

As the weeks and months passed, never having been used to really hard work, Captain Maximillem wondered just how long he would be able to go on. It was truly horrible, especially him realising this to possibly be the end of his piracy days. Again, he was to rue the day he had not made Jake the Snake walk the plank. Oh, if only! How he now longed to put the clock back!

It was several months later when early in the morning Captain Maximillem who was as usual busily breaking rocks, having briefly glanced out at the sea, caught sight of something familiar. Watched by guards, just before continuing his

work, managing a furtive look, to his dismay, fast approaching was a brightly coloured ship.

Realising possibly the brightly coloured ship to be the gaudy red ship belonging to his nemesis, "Captain du Plomp", he could only wonder what on earth he should be doing sailing these waters. Maybe, he had sold his ship with him now being with the island people, or had it been stolen?

Carrying on with his work to his alarm, he suddenly heard the sound of a familiar voice. Captain du Plomp in all his flamboyant dress had landed on the island with two of the island people. Captain Maximillem's thoughts were for him not to be spotted by him. Had he now come to laugh at him knowing he was here? He couldn't bear it. Oh, the humiliation!

Captain Maximillem immediately turned his back on Captain du Plomp who now deep in conversation with one of the guards, was handing something over to him. He hoped for him to very quickly go away but alas it was not going to happen. Along with two of his men happening to be working alongside him, the guard then gave the order for them to lay down their tools and follow him with Captain du Plomp to where close by, a jolly boat was moored up.

The three of them harnessed together then were frogmarched to the shore and ordered into the jolly boat. They were told they were going to help pull up a ship's anchor which was to have strangely somehow become stuck underneath the water. To Captain Maximillem this did seem to be very odd. Never had he heard such a thing.

Then after having reached Captain du Plomp's gaudy red ship, securing the jolly boat, all were to board her.

Releasing them from their bonds, but still threatening them with a sword, the guard gave orders for them to try pulling up the anchor. To their surprise, with very little effort, the anchor became dislodged. This left all now puzzled as to why they should ever have been needed?

It was not long however before all was revealed, for Captain du Plomp suddenly lurched out at the guard and pushed him overboard. All were left speechless, particularly Captain Maximillem, but quickly recovering from the shock it was now a case of all hands to the deck. Sighting the guard frantically swimming, getting nearer and nearer to the shore all he knew was that before very long an alarm would be raised. It was then without a moment to lose that the gaudy red ship was being sailed away as fast as she would go.

Captain du Plomp was beside himself with excitement! Standing at the helm of his ship he now felt himself a real pirate captain. But sadly, Captain Maximillem, although relieved and thankful for being rescued, in his mean-spirited fashion, still had a dislike of Captain du Plomp. Thinking him a real dandy as he always had done and never a real pirate captain, he now at the earliest opportunity was eager to leave the gaudy red ship.

Trying hard to be charming, thanking Captain du Plomp for rescuing him, he took the opportunity to enquire as to whether on his travels he had seen anything of his beloved ship the "Black Rigg".

Giving hope to Captain Maximillem, Captain du Plomp was able to inform him he thought his ship was to have passed him by only a day or so ago, heading in the direction they were now taking. He had called out to Captain Maximillem only to be told by a tall, thin raven-haired man there was a new captain on board owing to the old one having been caught smuggling and imprisoned.

It had been after this encounter purely by chance that Captain du Plomp sailing past the island through his telescope noticed a figure resembling Captain Maximillem. On seeing this, just in case it should have been him, he then hatched a plan to come to the rescue. In truth, it was and always had been that secretly Captain du Plomp hoped to learn from Captain Maximillem's expertise all about being a pirate captain.

Having been with the island people for a while, he had become restless, yearning to be back sailing the high seas once again seeking his fortune. And so, it was, with two of the island people and two pirates wishing to join him, he had set sail.

Hot on the trail of the Black Rigg

Captain Maximillem, very excited after having heard news about the Black Rigg having been sighted recently, now was most anxious for the ghastly gaudy coloured red ship he found himself on to sail as fast as she could. Almost forgetting he no longer captained a ship, he found it hard to stop himself giving orders to the crew to get a move on, which he did not. All left for him to do now was gently persuade Captain du Plomp to sail faster.

After sailing many days, seeing not a single ship let alone the Black Rigg, he was becoming very despondent. Would he ever see his beloved ship again, he was to often wonder? Just thinking about Jake the Snake pretending to be captain of his ship was making his blood boil so much he felt likely to explode! "Wait until I finally come across him," he was thinking to himself, "he shall pay dearly!"

Sailing for days on end, on board the gaudy red ship, was to reveal a few secrets about Captain du Plomp. Recounting his life story to Captain Maximillem, who listened intently, even though a lot of it he already knew. He was aware of Captain du Plomp's wealthy family, but had not known he sailed the seas looking for something more than riches. Leaving Captain Maximillem to wonder - whatever this could be? To him, finding treasure most certainly was all the happiness he ever looked for!

He was most surprised to be told by Captain du Plomp that he had not been happy with his privileged lifestyle. Having been sent to an expensive boarding school that he hated, leaving his parents at home, entertaining all sorts of important people and forever throwing grand parties and balls. Captain Maximillem did know, being told about how he had hated his French lessons, but was unaware of him being taught to become an accomplished swordsman.

Captain Maximillem also was to tell his tales about the giant green sea serpent he had met with on the high seas and of course, of "Ned" the ghostly pirate captain. This seemed to make Captain du Plomp feel a little unsettled. The thought of his ship being attacked by a giant sea serpent could surely be the end of him and encountering an eerie ghostly pirate, sent goose bumps down his neck.

Much to Captain Maximillem's annoyance, most evenings Captain du Plomp now played his musical instruments and was singing to the pirates who all unfortunately seemed to love it! Oh, how he couldn't wait to leave this ghastly ship! But, of course, he had no alternative but to sail on, in the hope that one day soon the "Black Rigg" would be spotted.

It was not too long before they were to spot in the distance, a ship - possibly the Black Rigg. Feeling a rush of excitement, Captain Maximillem's hope upon hope was for it to be the Black Rigg. He was so ready now to fight with Jake the Snake, even without having his long lost rusty old sword by his side. He would arm himself with whatever he could find and send Jake packing. No, he would have to make him walk the plank as that would sort him out once and for all!

Greatly disappointed finding it not to be the Black Rigg, Captain Maximillem suggested to Captain du Plomp that the ship should be plundered, anyway. Captain du Plomp, always very eager to prove himself a pirate captain, was then with the two island men, to set out in the jolly boat.

Reaching the ship, Captain du Plomp straightaway attempted to board her. But being met with much anger from the ship's crew, things did not go to plan. However, amongst the angry people who were ready to fight him off he noticed standing on the deck was a rather lovely young lady looking very alarmed and frightened.

After having seen the young lady Captain du Plomp now began speaking in his most charming voice, explaining to them he had meant no harm but had only come to ask if they could spare some food for some poor starving people. Upon hearing his explanation, the angry crew, assured of there being no danger, allowed Captain du Plomp to board the ship.

Once on board the ship, having left his men in the jolly boat, Captain du Plomp was very disappointed to find the lady had disappeared. However, he was not to wait long before she reappeared carrying with her what looked to be a large bundle of provisions. After having thanked all on board the ship and most particularly the young lady, all were to make their way back to the gaudy red ship.

Captain du Plomp just before clambering out of the jolly boat handed the bundle to Captain Maximillem, anxiously awaiting the treasure. Well pleased with the size of the bag, excitedly he hurriedly opened it, but what he was to find inside caused him to cry out in alarm. "What's this, what's this?" he began shouting crossly, "Where's the treasure?" It was then that Captain du Plomp in a dreamy sort of way went on to explain to him exactly what had happened.

After hearing what Captain du Plomp had to say, Captain Maximillem was absolutely horrified. Never ever had he heard such nonsense! That he should have been so silly, all because of a pretty lady! The sooner he thought to himself I get off this ghastly ship and back to being captain of the Black Rigg, the better!

It has to be said that although Captain Maximillem disliked Captain du Plomp's gaudy red ship immensely, he secretly would have to admit to it being comfortable. Compared to the Black Rigg, probably owing to Captain du Plomp's fussy ways, she did seem to be smart. There too was the added bonus of her being stocked with an abundance of supplies, most importantly, plenty of rum and ale.

Journeying on many more weeks with Captain du Plomp, always at the back of Captain Maximillem's mind was "would he ever be reunited with the Black Rigg? So far there had been not a single sighting of a ship to look anything like her. He made sure that after Captain du Plomp's recent nonsense he and his men always went to plunder any passing ships themselves. Having met more than a few ships to plunder, Captain du Plomp with this arrangement, left in charge of his ship, did not mind one little bit, he was only too pleased to receive any treasure!

Ladies aboard the Gaudy Red Ship!

Whilst continuing their search for the Black Rigg sailing on the high seas they were to meet some dangerous situations. Due to Captain Maximillem's past experiences, having met more than a few ferocious storms, it was owing to his expertise that thankfully he was able to save the gaudy red ship from too much damage. There had been one or two hair-raising moments though, with seas thrashing so violently over the decks to almost have caused the gaudy red ship to capsize. But thankfully they seemed to now be heading for warmer climes with it all being calm.

As well as anxiously looking for the Black Rigg, Captain Maximillem was on the lookout for the giant, green serpent that had almost sunk his ship damaging her so badly. He was thankful that so far there were no sightings recorded. Of course, although he was secretly grateful for Captain du Plomp to have rescued him, he still had some mean thoughts about him. Wondering how he would behave should the serpent suddenly appear, he did rather think it would be in a most cowardly fashion!

After many disappointments, sighting ships and finding them not to be the Black Rigg, and very often too far away to bother setting out to plunder them, Captain Maximillem looking out to sea was to suddenly notice a very small boat not far away, bobbing around in the water. Quick to alert Captain du Plomp, who now peering through his telescope, was to let out an excited cry. He had seen two ladies in the boat, one of them frantically waving to them.

Hearing this, Captain Maximillem's thoughts were to just carry on sailing straight past them. Telling Captain du Plomp he thought ladies should never ever be allowed on a pirate ship, as they only bring bad luck.

But Captain du Plomp, captain of his ship, and also being a ladies' man, had other ideas. Full of excitement he shouted to Captain Maximillem to hurry and throw the ladies a rope. Before he had any chance to do this though, alerted to something going on, upon seeing the ladies others now had quickly rushed forward to lend a hand.

Seeing the ladies on a pirate ship was all too much for Captain Maximillem to bear. It was most unfortunate however that he was to let his feeling known leaving the ladies in no doubt that they were not welcome. But his behaviour only infuriated Captain du Plomp who immediately ordered him down below decks.

Although he was not to stay below deck very long, having been sent there did cause Captain Maximillem great embarrassment. "Mark my words, mark my words, much ill luck will now befall this ghastly ship," he was grumbling to himself, "and the sooner I get off her the better!"

The two ladies, one an heiress, a true beauty, the other her maid, slightly rounded with a handsome kindly face, Captain Maximillem hoped, were not to be staying very long with them.

After having recovered slightly from their ordeal and partaken in a little food and drink, the ladies' story was soon to unravel.

They began by recounting how late at night a pirate named, "Sam", feeling sorry for them had helped them to escape in a small boat from a pirate ship where they were being held captive. They had been kidnapped one sultry evening whilst strolling along the quayside.

It was soon to become noticeable that the maid named, "Bessie", whenever addressing the heiress was calling her, "My Lady". It was then the heiress was to reveal her name to be "Lady Sophia Greystone". Having heard this, Captain Maximillem found it a bit strange Captain du Plomp did not seem all that impressed. This being probably due to his privileged upbringing - he was well used to meeting grand persons.

To Captain Maximillem's disdain, now Captain du Plomp, whenever engaged in conversation with the Lady Sophia, was behaving in a somewhat soppy fashion. Witnessing this only confirmed what he already thought of him. He also was playing his flute to her and singing. UGRR!

Half listening to what the ladies were saying, Captain Maximillem's ears suddenly pricked up. Unable to believe what he was hearing, he now listened intently to every word. From the description given of a pirate ship and its captain, from whom they had escaped, it could only have been the "Black Rigg" and "Jake the Snake!"

Eager to hear whatever else was being said, he now was able to ascertain Lady Sophia after having been seized, was being held for ransom, and the ship was heading in a southerly direction towards her parents' estate.

Captain du Plomp hearing all this was to immediately order his ship be turned round and head south. He hoped with Captain Maximillem's expertise in locating the Black Rigg with Jake the Snake, it could well be enough to prove his worthiness to the family of Lady Sophia. Captain du Plomp now realised himself to be hopelessly in love!

Hot on the trail of the Black Rigg with Jake the Snake, the gaudy red ship now was sailing as fast as she could. Leaving Captain Maximillem to scan the seas in the hope of a sighting of his ship with Captain du Plomp doing what he does best, entertaining the ladies!

At long last a Sighting!

The ladies, much to the dismay of Captain Maximillem, but the delight of Captain du Plomp, after several weeks, were still on board the gaudy red ship.

Having met with the odd storm, with it having been all hands to the deck, Lady Sophia and Bessie were turning out to be surprisingly stalwart in spite of their predicament. Bessie, in particular, whilst attempting to thaw Captain Maximillem, who was having none of it, had been trying her best, spoiling him with her delicious recipes. It was all to no avail though, for as far as he was concerned women never, ever should be on a pirate ship. No, even if deep down he did seem to think Bessie rather comely and a kind soul.

It was then at last that early one morning they were to see just coming into view on the horizon the familiar sight of a black ship! Greatly excited, Captain Maximillem wanted to have a jolly boat launched immediately, only to be persuaded by Captain du Plomp it was wiser to wait until darkness fell, then launch an attack under cover, surprising them.

It was fortunate that the gaudy red ship being small, hopefully, would not be recognised by Jake the Snake to be a pirate ship. It too seemed lucky there had been no attempt made to plunder it. Maybe they were just resting up?

Awaiting the dark that day for Captain Maximillem was agony. It could not come soon enough. However, this was to give him plenty of time to work out just how and what he was going to do to Jake the Snake. All sorts of thoughts had been circling around in his head. He could keep him captive in a cage below deck before making him walk the plank. That seemed an excellent idea. Or maybe he would just throw him overboard whenever there were any large sharks or whales spotted. But then it was to suddenly come to him. He had remembered a long time ago once visiting a most unpleasant island. Yes, that would be a very nice place for Jake the Snake to pay a visit to!

At last the wait was over! Night had finally fallen. For an excited Captain Maximillem, making sure the Black Rigg still to be in position, as he had done regularly, it did come as a surprise when Captain du Plomp insisted on accompanying him. After handing Captain Maximillem one of his old swords, in great excitement he was now waving high in the air one of his own very fine swords. In truth, he had never taken part in a real fight before, but the very thought of doing so was making him become quite overwhelmed with excitement.

Grateful for the loan of the sword, having lost his own rusty old one a while ago, after checking the Black Rigg still to be in position, Captain Maximillem, two of his men with two of the island people clambered into the jolly boat awaiting Captain du Plomp to join them.

Much to Captain Maximillem's annoyance at having been kept waiting, finally he appeared with Lady Sophia on his arm. Bidding her a fond farewell, much to Captain Maximillem's disgust, kisses flying through the air, they were at last to set off.

Quietly making their way in a sea remaining calm, the only sounds to be heard were that of the sea gently lapping the sides of their boat. Guiding them towards the Black Rigg they had with them a small faint lantern, which now almost reaching her, very quickly was extinguished.

Undetected, with no sounds heard or there being any movement on board the Black Rigg, even with the almost full moon that once in a while had been peeping out from behind the clouds, their mission it seemed had been accomplished!

Having sneaked up on the Black Rigg, one by one, Captain Maximillem first to attempt boarding the Black Rigg, followed by Captain du Plomp and two island people, all managed to board the ship. Having quickly looked around and seeing no signs of life it was much to Captain du Plomp's alarm that Captain Maximillem, unable to contain himself any longer, had now begun shouting for Jake the Snake to show himself.

It was not long before Jake the Snake, having armed himself and still half asleep, appeared on deck. To see him again now turned Captain Maximillem's face a puce colour with his sharp, tiny eyes growing darker and darker. Taking the sword loaned to him by Captain du Plomp, without any hesitation he began lunging forth at him. Then a ferocious sword fight took place.

Disappointed to not be involved in the fight, Captain du Plomp instead decided just in case any of Jake the Snake's men were to try to intervene, he would scare them off waving his sword high in the air, at the same time letting them see a really mean steely look across his face.

He need not have worried. Having been aroused from their sleep and hearing noises coming from up on deck, most of the crew appeared. But there was something rather odd about them. None were attempting to assist their captain. It almost seemed they were hoping for him to be taken captive.

Triumphantly, Captain Maximillem won the fight and with the help of Captain du Plomp with his men, Jake the Snake all tussled up, was dumped well down below decks.

Having taken back the Black Rigg, Captain Maximillem now had to decide what he should do with Jake the Snake's men. Soon back in grumpy pirate captain mode, his first thought was that the traitors should be left on the very next island they came across.

Gradually, however, Jake the Snake's men began relating their stories. One told how he made two men walk the plank, all because being so tired with all the tasks set them, they complained! Another told of how they all almost had starved, being punished for not owning up to helping themselves to ale on a sweltering hot day. And so it was, many more stories were told, each one worse than the one before.

It too was disclosed there was a pirate named Sam left tied up well below decks awaiting somewhere suitable for him to walk the plank owing to him having allowed some ladies to escape. Of course, hearing this, Captain du Plomp did not hesitate to have him released immediately.

Captain du Plomp anxious now to return to Lady Sophia, to take her safely back to her home suggested Captain Maximillem threaten the men with either walking the plank or swearing their allegiance to him. Rarely heeding to any advice, knowing the urgent need of a crew, Captain Maximillem actually thought this to be a good idea! It was then, of course, without any hesitation all the men very sensibly chose to sign their allegiance to him.

Soon they were to bid farewell. Captain Maximillem, still of the opinion of his being a dandy, and most certainly not a pirate captain, it was fair to say, was grateful for having been saved. Their farewell, although it was not exactly a fond one did turn out to be an amicable one. Neither knowing whether they would ever meet again.

Setting sail the first thing Captain Maximillem intended to do was head towards an island he knew very well. Reaching the island several days later he then ordered the Black Rigg be sailed as near as possible.

Close to the island, with help from the two pirates seeking vengeance after their imprisonment with him, Jake the Snake was released from his bounds then led up on deck. And so it was, that with all the other pirates sheepishly looking on, Jake the Snake walked the plank.

The last seen of Jake the Snake was him frantically swimming, almost having reached the island. Just to imagine his surprise and horror upon setting foot on the island to be greeted by giant rats bringing a rare chuckle to Captain Maximillem.

Back in command with his two men and half a dozen of Jake the Snake's, enabled him to at long last carry on as he always had done. Sailing the high seas endlessly searching for his treasure, to be found hidden on an island, but more often when plundering ships. Learning from Jake the Snake's captaincy, not to risk ever having to walk the plank, he did think that maybe he should try looking after his men a little better.

Being back at sea was not without its problems for the Black Rigg. So far there had been another sighting of Ned the ghostly pirate captain, warning them of eminent danger, along with, thankfully, a distant sighting of the giant green serpent, from which they then made a very hasty retreat. But there were some happy moments too, especially when after plundering a ship they found an excellent haul of riches.

After all that had happened to him, Captain Maximillem did not attempt very often to visit shore. On the rare occasion he did, heavily disguised as a vagabond, he now made sure he kept well away from taverns. For not only was he a pirate captain, but was now an escaped prisoner – a wanted man!

As to what happened to Captain du Plomp? Captain Maximillem never did see or hear from him again. Maybe he was to have found happiness with Lady Sophia's parents agreeing to the match. After all he never truly was a pirate captain and was to have rescued their daughter from the clutches of a dastardly pirate.

Lightning Source UK Ltd.
Milton Keynes UK
UKHW020007100522
402711UK00009B/2244